# ARTHUR'S READING RACE

## 识字大赢家

（美）马克·布朗　绘著

范晓星　译

CHISO 新疆青少年出版社

Arthur learned to read
in school.

3

Now Arthur reads everywhere!

He reads in the car.

He reads in bed.

He reads

to his puppy, Pal.

Arthur even reads

to his little sister, D.W.

One day Arthur said,

"I can teach YOU to read, too."

"I already know how to read,"

said D.W.

"You do not!" said Arthur.

"Do too!" said D.W.

"Prove it," said Arthur.

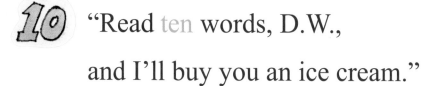 "Read ten words, D.W.,

and I'll buy you an ice cream."

D.W. stuck out her hand.

"It's a deal," she said.

"Let's go!"

They raced to the park.

Arthur pointed to a sign.

"What's that say?" he asked.

"Zoō," said D.W.

"Easy as pie."

9

# 3

"I spy three words,"

said Arthur.

"Me too," said D.W.

"Taxi, gas, milk."

Arthur stepped off the curb.

"Look out!" said D.W.

"It says Don't Walk.

You could get hit by a car."

"All right,
Miss Smarty-Pants,
what's that say?"
asked Arthur.

"Police," said D.W.
"And you better
keep off the grass
or the police will get you."

15

"Bank," said D.W.

"I have a bank.

I hide my money in it

so you can't find it.

Bank makes eight words."

"We're almost home,"
said Arthur.
"Too bad.
You only read eight words.
No ice cream
for you today."

"Hold your horses," said D.W.

"I spy…ice cream.

Hot dog! I read ten words.

Let's eat!"

pizza chip | shoe lace

Bumpy road | moose ripple

frog chip

egg shell

D.W. and Arthur ran

to the ice cream store.

Arthur bought two big cones.

20

Strawberry for D.W.

and chocolate for himself.

"Yummy," said D.W.

Arthur sat down.

"Sit down with me," said Arthur,

"and I'll read you my book."

"No," said D.W.

"I'll read YOU the book."

Arthur shook his head.

"I don't think so," he said.

"There are too many words

that you don't know."

D.W. laughed.

"Get up, Arthur."

"Now I can teach you

two words that you don't know,"

said D.W.

"WET PAINT!"

24

3. 亚瑟在学校学会了认字。

4. 现在，亚瑟走到哪儿读到哪儿！
他在汽车上读，
在床上读，
给小狗宝儿读，

5. 还给自己的小妹妹朵拉读。

6. 一天，亚瑟对朵拉说："我来教你读书吧。"

"我已经会读书了。"朵拉回答。

"你不会！"亚瑟说。
"我会！"朵拉回答。

7. "那你证明给我看。"亚瑟说，"朵拉，要是你能认出十个词语，我就给你买一个冰激凌。"

朵拉伸出手来说："说话算话。"
"走吧。"亚瑟回应。

8. 他们跑到公园。
亚瑟指着一个标示牌问："那上面写的什么字？"

"动物园！"朵拉回答，"这也太简单了。"

10. "我看见三个词语。"亚瑟说。

11. "我也看见了，"朵拉回应，"出租车、加油站、牛奶。"

12. 亚瑟迈下路阶。

"小心！"朵拉说，"路灯上写着'行人止步'，小心被车撞到！"

14. "好吧，机灵鬼小姐，那上面写的是什么？"亚瑟问。

15. "警察，"朵拉回答，"你最好快点离开草地，不然警察就来抓你啦。"

16. "看，银行，"朵拉说，"我也有个小存钱罐。

17. "我把我的零钱放在里面，好让你找不到它们。算上'银行'，我已经认出八个词语啦。"

18. "快到家了，"亚瑟说，"真可惜，你只认出了八个词语，今天不能给你买冰激凌喽。"

19. "别忙嘛，"朵拉说，"我看到了……冰激凌，还有热狗！我认出十个词语啦，咱们吃冰激凌去吧！"

20. 朵拉和亚瑟跑进冰激凌店。
亚瑟买了两个大蛋筒冰激凌。

21. 亚瑟把草莓味儿的给了朵
拉，自己留下巧克力味儿的。
　　"太好吃了！"朵拉咂咂嘴说。

30

22. 亚瑟坐下来说："坐我旁边吧，我来给你读书。"

"不，"朵拉说，"我来给你读。"

23. 亚瑟摇摇头回答：

"不行，这本书里有很多你不认识的字。"

朵拉"扑哧"一笑，说：

"快起来，亚瑟！"

24. "还是我来给你读四个你不认识的字吧，"朵拉说，"油漆未干！"